W9-BGX-653

Ex-Library: Friends of

ANDY'S
PIRATE SHIP

ANDY'S
PIRATE SHIP

Philippe Dupasquier

Henry Holt and Company · New York

ANDY'S PIRATE SHIP

A Spot-the-Difference Book

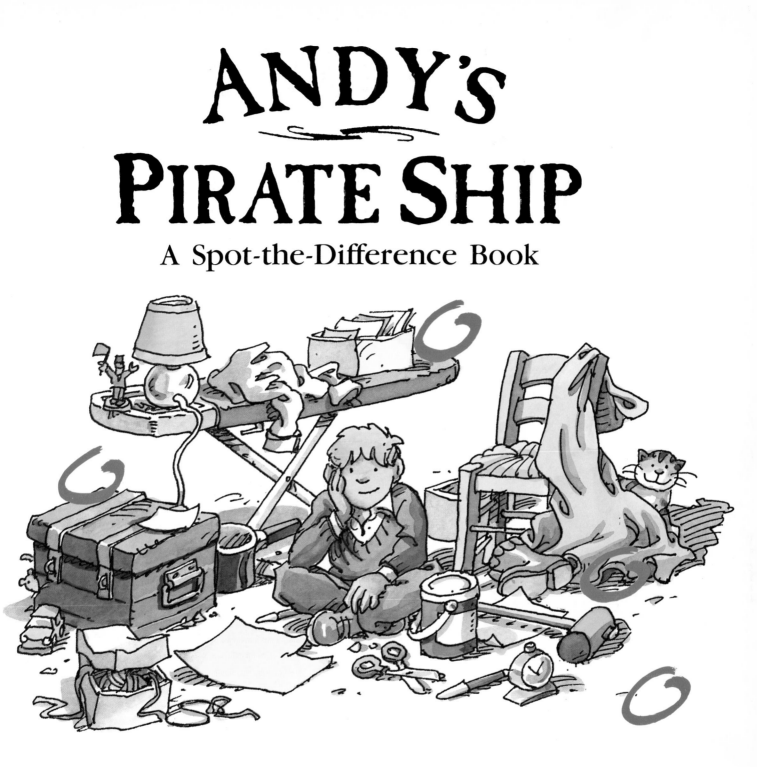

Philippe Dupasquier

Henry Holt and Company · New York

LAKE COUNTY PUBLIC LIBRARY

3 3113 01396 9102

Henry Holt and Company, Inc.
Publishers since 1866
115 West 18th Street, New York, New York 10011
Henry Holt is a registered trademark of Henry Holt and Company, Inc.
Copyright © 1994 by Philippe Dupasquier. All rights reserved.
First published in the United States in 1994 by Henry Holt and Company, Inc.
Published in Canada by Fitzhenry & Whiteside Ltd., 195 Allstate Parkway, Markham, Ontario L3R 4T8.
Originally published in Great Britain in 1994 by Andersen Press under the title *Tom's Pirate Ship*.

Library of Congress Catalog Card Number 93-79311

ISBN 0-8050-3154-5
First American Edition—1994
Printed in Italy
1   3   5   7   9   10   8   6   4   2

Andy was bored with all his games and toys. He was even bored with T.V.

I wish I had a pirate ship to play with, he thought. Then he had a brilliant idea. "I'll make one myself," he said.

"All I need to do is to pick up a few things from around the house. I know just where to start," he said, and he opened the storeroom door.

He found two things he could use for a pirate ship—one of
them would make a perfect mast.

Next, Andy went into the laundry room. It was always a
terrible mess and there were plenty of things to choose from.

He took five things altogether—two of them made a pair.

The kitchen was right next to the laundry room. It smelled great in there. His mom had just made some cupcakes.

He took one cupcake for himself as well as four things for his pirate ship.

Then Andy went into the garage.

"There it is," he said, when he saw the police car he thought he had lost.

"But that's not what I need right now," he said, and he took four more things for his pirate ship.

Andy went around to the back of the house. He wondered what he might find in the yard.

He collected six things for his ship.

Now he had twenty-one pirate ship parts. A nice beginning, but it wasn't enough. He went upstairs to his sister's bedroom.

Andy wasn't supposed to touch anything belonging to his sister. But he needed more plunder. He took four things altogether. One of them would look great on a pirate's shoulder.

When Andy got to his own bedroom he remembered that his mother had asked him to clean it up.

But he had no time for that now. He took nine objects for his pirate ship—six of them looked very much the same.

Andy was on a roll. He knew there would be lots of interesting things in his parents' study.

He took five things altogether.

Finally Andy went up to the attic. It was full of hundreds of
different things. There was a broken television, a pair of skis, and
the high chair that Andy had used when he was a baby.

There were also lots of old fashioned things like his grandfather's phonograph, a top hat, and an old sword that Andy's dad said had been used in a famous battle.

This time Andy took only three things for his pirate ship. At last he had everything he wanted.

And what a ship he built!

THE STOREROOM

1 box

1 broom

THE LAUNDRY ROOM

1 pair of boots

1 umbrella

1 T-shirt

1 coat hanger

THE KITCHEN

1 banana

2 spoons

1 dish towel

THE GARAGE

1 ball of string

1 shoe box

1 flowerpot

1 wheel

THE BACKYARD

3 clothespins

1 croquet mallet

1 umbrella stand

1 handkerchief

ANDY'S SISTER'S BEDROOM

1 parrot

1 T-shirt

1 belt

1 felt-tip pen

ANDY'S BEDROOM

6 bowling pins

1 teddy bear

1 rocket

1 section of
railroad track

ANDY'S PARENTS' STUDY

1 pair of scissors

1 roll of masking tape

1 sheet of newspaper

1 ruler

1 piece of white paper

THE ATTIC

1 chandelier

1 broken doll

1 curtain

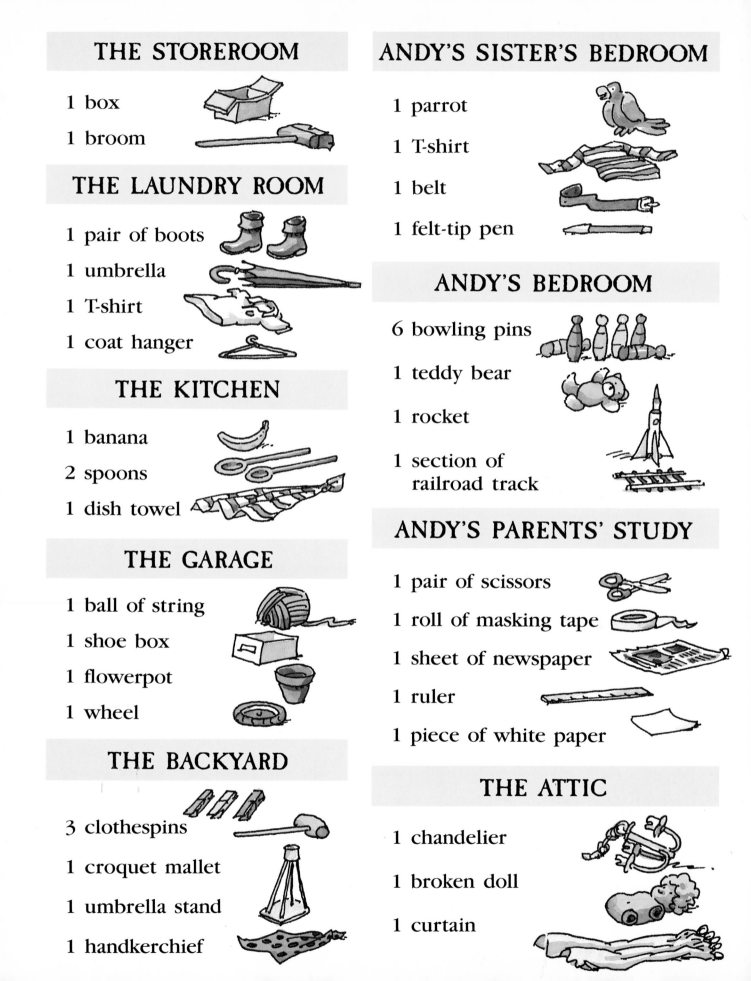

Andy knew he'd get in trouble if he didn't return all the things he had taken, so he made a list of where everything came from. Coming up with the name for his ship wasn't easy, but he found something in each room that helped.

He also thought it would be a good idea
to note some things he came across that might
come in handy on his next project.
Can you find the mouse and tennis ball
in each picture?

THE STOREROOM

1 candle
1 paint roller
3 spiders
1 cane
1 football

THE GARAGE

1 skateboard
1 apple core
1 funnel
1 pair of oars
1 sledgehammer

ANDY'S BEDROOM

1 telephone
1 paper boat
1 snake
1 butterfly net
1 cork

THE LAUNDRY ROOM

1 sponge
1 frog
1 boat
1 loose button
2 pairs of rubber gloves

THE BACKYARD

1 flag
1 kite
7 animals
1 rake
1 straw

ANDY'S PARENTS' STUDY

1 calculator
1 rubber band
1 box of matches
1 thumb tack
1 paper clip

THE KITCHEN

Half a lemon
1 snail
1 elephant
1 oven mitt
1 knife

ANDY'S SISTER'S BEDROOM

1 giraffe
1 chair
3 rabbits
1 saddle
1 car

THE ATTIC

1 shepherd
3 light bulbs
1 umbrella
1 padlock
1 jack-in-the-box

Ex-Library: Friends of
Lake County Public Library

JUV P DUPA   FF
Dupasquier, Philippe.
Andy's pirate ship

LAKE COUNTY PUBLIC LIBRARY
INDIANA

AD	FEB 0 4 '95 FF	MU
AV	GR	NC
BO	HI	SJ
CL	HO	CN L
DS	LS	

No AR

THIS BOOK IS RENEWABLE BY PHONE OR IN PERSON IF THERE IS NO RESERVE
WAITING OR FINE DUE.
                                        LCP #0390